# THE BAGGAGE CARRIERS

Writing from Center for Independence
of the Disabled, New York

NY WRITERS COALITION PRESS
SPRING 2019

Editor: Avra Wing
Interior Layout & Design: Nicole Di Luccio
Cover Image: Erwan Hesry

*The Baggage Carriers* is a collection of writing and art from NY Writers Coalition's workshop at Center for Independence of the Disabled, New York, in Manhattan.

NY Writers Coalition Press, Inc.
80 Hanson Place, Suite 604
Brooklyn, NY 11217
(718) 398-2883
info@nywriterscoalition.org
www.nywriterscoalition.org

# Contents

## *The Baggage Carriers*

# THE BAGGAGE

# CARRIERS

# Introduction

This book marks the 10th anniversary of NY Writers Coalition's workshop at the Center for the Independence of the Disabled, New York (CIDNY). Some of the people represented here have been with the group from the very beginning, or almost the beginning. Others have come for several years. A few have joined fairly recently. Each person brings a unique energy and creativity to the group. We have had members leave for various reasons—work, moving, illness—but we always think of them as still being part of our community. The saddest loss we've had was the death of Joe Rosenbaum in 2012. Joe had been a key part of the workshop for a long time. He was a terrific writer and a gentle soul loved by all. For those of us who knew him, his absence is felt every time we enter the room. We continue on, with Joe always in our hearts.

Each week when we meet, I am surprised by the variety and quality of the work that is produced by the participants. We write in two 20-minutes sessions, and in that short amount of time, incredibly imaginative and beautiful poems and stories are created. Each person has a distinct voice that we look forward to hearing. The pieces sometimes make us laugh, sometimes profoundly move us, and always impress us with their strength.

The title, *The Baggage Carriers*, refers to the different kinds of emotional and physical burdens we all carry. This is especially resonant for our group, because many of the members have disabilities. But every person, of whatever abilities, is a baggage carrier. We all have some pain, some trouble in our lives.

I have been privileged to be the leader of the CIDNY workshop for the entire 10 years of its existence. Every week is a joyful experience, sitting around the table, schmoozing, listening to the words of good writers, hearing the appreciative comments of the members on each other's work, getting to spend time with so many wonderful people. It has certainly enriched my life, and I hope that all those who have been in the workshop, past and present, feel the same way.

I am also grateful to be part of the NY Writers Coalition. The staff and my fellow workshop leaders do incredible work and are, without exception, talented, warm, generous and genuine. I want to give a special shout-out to Nicole Di Luccio, who did all the heavy lifting of the "baggage" to produce this book.

CIDNY, as well, deserves to be praised here. The organization, Margi Trapani in particular, has graciously hosted us for a decade. I am proud to be associated in some small way with people who so forcefully and effectively advocate for the rights of people with disabilities.

It is my great pleasure to be able to celebrate the 10th anniversary of the CIDNY workshop by sharing some of the work of our members.

AVRA WING

Workshop Leader, CIDNY

Spring 2019

*Harriet W. Andrade*

♦

## The Feldman Saga
*("A Busy Social Season")*
*("Joan Levine Returns")*

The phone rang in the Feldman's oak-paneled den. Nathan Feldman, who was home for the weekend from Ohio State, wasn't quick enough to answer it, absorbed as he was in his geometry textbook. This was the last course that Nathan needed for his bachelor's degree, and he had failed it once.

"Why waste your money, Dad," Nathan had reasoned with his father. "I'm going into business with you, which is what we wanted."

Harry Feldman always answered in his unique Russian Jewish accent, "You vill FINISH your education, Nathan. You vill need that degree to be respected." Harry Feldman, owner and president of Thrifty Linen and Towel, certainly got his way.

The Feldmans were having a busy social calendar. Nathan's mother, Sarah Feldman, and his fiancée, Estelle Rashnakov, were shopping in downtown Dayton for Estelle's trousseau. Harry Feldman was meeting with Mr. Conklin at the Winterly National Bank building. Mr. Conklin, Winterly's president, was still trying to persuade Harry to take some foreclosure properties off the bank's hands. Now, in the fall of 1952, postwar Daytonians were not all thriving like the Feldmans or the Torversons in the big federal house down the hill.

"Mr. Conklin, I appreciate vat you trust me. But I don't

**17**

vant to profit from other people's misery," was Harry Feldman's answer so far. Nevertheless, Harry took great pride in Mr. Conklin's good opinion.

Nathan mulled over these thoughts as he bounded down the carpeted stairs from his cedar-paneled attic bedroom. Nathan hoped the phone wouldn't ring anymore. He was on his way to the factory on Meachum Street to assist his cousin Jack with loading the clean linen supplies onto the trucks.

If Nathan's older sister Hillary was still at home, she would be doing the woman's stuff like answering the phone and taking messages. Nathan's big sis and her husband, Alan, were overloaded at their rented rooms in St. Louis. Ex-POW Alan's job at WKSL Radio was shaky, as the advertising revenue was not picking up. Nathan's little nephew, baby Irving, was colicky. Hillary was tired of typing envelopes at home on her college Remington. At least she mastered a practical skill before she dropped out of Ohio State to marry Alan Feinberg. Nathan learned the truth in his secret calls to Hillary from the payphone at Barshay's Malts and Lunch downtown, where Nathan's best friend Lennie Barshay worked part-time for his father, Sy.

How long could Hillary and Alan hold on to their stubborn pride before the head of the family, Harry Feldman, set out for Dayton's Union Station with his Samsonite tan leather suitcase and his Winterly Bank checkbook to rescue them?

Nathan had just let Lola Swanson in through the breakfast nook entrance. She traveled from West Dayton and walked from the bus stop at Oak and State streets. "Morning, Mr. Nathan."

"Good morning, Lola. Mother left a list for you on the

counter when you're ready."

Lola thanked Nathan, then went straight to the finished basement, where she removed her overcoat and placed it in the maid's closet. She took her soft work shoes out of her shopping bag, changed into them, and briskly climbed the stairs to retrieve Sarah Feldman's list and start her household chores.

As Nathan was taking a quick gulp of freshly squeezed orange juice from one of the everyday breakfast glasses, the phone in the den rang again. Nathan went to answer it, deciding to make it short so he could get over to the factory.

"Some of the trip was choppy, Nathan. But the SS United States was fabulous! Mother and I adored Paris. We toured with a guide and saw all the sites like in a movie. We shopped at Printemps and had coffee at Café de la Paix, we saw the artists in Montmartre . . . There's poverty, too, Nathan. Those poor French urchins in the back streets ...."

"I'm glad you're home safely, Joanie. Give my regards to your parents."

"By the way, Nathan, we hope to see you soon with Sarah and Harry at The Blue Tondelayo," Joan Levine urged. The Blue Tondelayo was her father Les Levine's lobster restaurant on South Salem Road. It was a Hollywood reinvention of a Pacific island and very popular in Dayton and the surrounding towns among those who could afford to dine there. Les Levine was also a good customer at Thrifty Linen and Towel, which Nathan and Joan's broken engagement had not spoiled for their fathers.

"My fiancée Estelle is looking forward to meeting you, Joanie."

"My very best wishes, Nathan," Joan Levine said. "All the health, happiness and success in the world."

"I know you really mean it, Joanie."

"We just found out a couple of days ago, Nathan. Mother and I had barely gotten home when Sylvia Schleier called."

Nathan thought back to that incident last year at the Charm Beauty Salon. If Joanie Levine hadn't been upset about the shade of red that hairdresser Connie Twardzik applied to Joan's long, thick hair, and if it hadn't been raining, the Janover Jewelers four carat round diamond would be on Joan's hand today, instead of Estelle Rashnakov's. Although Connie Twardzik had to be treated by a doctor, she generously chose not press a police complaint when Joan hit her on the head with an umbrella.

"It's been good talking to you, Joanie. I'd better get going to the factory. My cousin Jack really needs me over there."

"Always the diligent worker, Nathan."

"Some lucky guy is out there waiting for you, Joanie. I've got to get going."

"See you soon, Nathan."

Nathan grabbed his plaid work jacket from the breakfast nook closet. Lola was methodically wiping down kitchen surfaces. She held the sponge and Bon Ami container in her rubber-gloved hands. Nathan knew his mother appreciated Lola's neatness and efficiency. Nathan perceived that Lola was a refined and lovely young woman.

"Mother and Estelle will be home soon," Nathan called out to Lola as he left through the breakfast nook door. Lola gestured with a small wave and smile and continued working.

Nathan pulled out of the gravel driveway in his 1951 Studebaker two-door sedan. He hoped that Dad would okay a new car this year. As Nathan understood his father's booming business, he knew they could certainly afford two or three new cars in upcoming 1953. Nathan could hear in his mind Harry Feldman's voice, cautioning in his Russian Jewish accent, "Ve don't show off in Dayton, Ohio."

Just as Nathan turned the ignition, he recognized his mother's 1950 mint green Chevy Bel Air coming up the hill. Sarah Feldman was at the wheel, with her soon-to-be daughter-in-law Estelle beside her. Nathan made a smart guess that the trunk would be piled with boxes from the exclusive Sydna Shop.

**End of Episode**

♦

# *Untitled 1*

A haircut in Chinatown
costs me 6 dollars.
I don't speak Chinese,
but my liberal arts education
gave me the gift of diplomacy.
One may find Amy Tan books
in the library
next to Puerto Rican books.
A eulogy for Puerto Rico:
I love Mommi.
I love Poppi.
They came to America
in a tin cup airplane.

# *Untitled 2*

NYC is filled
with famous people
and gangsters.
You need to be brave
to live in NYC.
Heaven is a city
like NYC.

## Untitled 3

Johnny goes fishing
on the waterfront.
He is amazingly
handsome.
When I see him
I see me.
I need a good hobby.
Romance is my hobby.
But sometimes
I get into trouble.

## Untitled 4

Catholics believe
we may pray for our deceased.
Not sure of the validity
but the practice is soothing.
My deceased appear in my dreams.
My dreams are like foreign films.
If I write about my deceased
in Spanish
they are sweeter and lovable.
If I write in Spanish
my shadows are beautiful.
My deceased are in solitary
because I refuse to let them escape
from my dreams.

## *Untitled 5*

My melancholy may kiss
any blessing into a curse.
Then I pray all day.
Melancholy is a harmless companion.
Makes you into a saint.
Unlike real darkness.

*Philip Bennett*

♦

# *A Settling*
### *(excerpted from* The Piper's Tune*)*

A wind whistles and rattles through a loose windowpane. A shutter groans, a blackened chandelier tinkles, sways, barely visible in the dark dining hall, which is lit by a single candle.

Samhain Hall lowers the long wooden pipe from his smooth lips to tighten his ragged scarf and knit cap over his thick reddish hair. He takes another small swig from his bottle of cheap ale and returns it to the small wooden table.

Easy there, he thinks. Don't know where to piss around here.

He settles back into the filthy cushioned easy chair and continues to improvise his Irish aire. The sweet tune drifts through the bleak large room. Shadows cast by the flickering candle dance against the grimy grey walls. Once the dining area for the crowded hundreds of patients who lived and died in this monstrous London house over 200 years ago, now there is no evidence of a single living thing ever being here, not even a cobweb. All the furniture is in place, exactly as Samhain remembers it, now covered with two centuries of dust. He repeatedly stops to wipe his fingers on his baggy pants. My sister never was very tidy, he thinks. Seems being a ghost didn't give her much educating.

Samhain knows it's Nellie's ghost they talk about around town, keeping almost everyone away all these years and almost killing those who tried staying here or tearing the place down. Not very sociable, are you, Nell?, Samhain thinks. And who can blame you, after what I did to you? Somebody should pay. Should be me. Should end with me. It's been 286 bloody years, too long, stuff won't let me die. She can end this. Spirits have that power, more powerful than this bloody stuff. Then I'll take her burden, damn my eyes.

Samhain blows four more twisted notes, pauses, then plays a tune his grandmother Cathleen taught her grandchildren, saved only in the Annals. She'll know this, he thinks. Nobody else living knows this one. All long dead. I should be, too. Tonight's the night.

Another moan. Maybe nothing. He keeps playing. The room grows chilly. More moaning, ending with a hushed, echoed gasp, then starts again. He stops playing, stands up. "Nellie," he speaks plainly in Irish Gaelic. "It's Samhain. Sammy. I'm here to take your place in hell, release you to paradise. Nellie, can you hear me? Nellie? I hurt you to your soul. I made you cry and suffer. You're in hell because of me. Please, sweet Nell, send me now to Hell forever and ascend to your proper place in the next world.

A shutter slams hard against a window frame. The moan grows angry, weepy. Samhain feels the floor vibrate.

"Nellie, stop trying to scare me! Don't you understand I want to die? I deserve hell! Nellie!"

The quarter-full ale bottle slides off the short table and lands hard on his foot. "Shite!" he curses under his breath, then quickly bends down to save the liquid. The bottle flies into his face, breaking his nose. Staggering backwards, he trips on the thin carpet. Coughing in the dust, scrambling to his feet, he hears a piercing shriek. Not a dream. Nose still broken. Another windless blast of cold. "Nellie! You can't chase me away! Just send me to hell! Set yourself free!"

Another shriek. The little table streaks into his gut. The ale bottle explodes into sharp pieces that impale themselves into his swollen face.

"AAARRRRCH! Nellie! Still not leaving! You'll have to kill me! Try harder! Take your revenge! Nellie!"

He hears a chorus of guttural wailings and moans from upstairs. "Is that where you are, Nell? I'm coming, Nell!"

Samhain easily finds the wide, solid carpeted staircase. Halfway up, the carpet rises up in a wave, throwing him backwards. He tumbles down, lays there unable to breathe or speak. At last, he thinks as he passes out. Then wakes. No hurt, feel fine. Damn my eyes! "Nell, still not dead! You must kill me to make yourself free!"

He struggles to his feet. The moanings have become hoarse angry wails. A ceiling board drops on his head, cracking his skull.

He slowly picks himself up. "It's not working, Nell! Let me come to you! We have to find a way!" An old kerosene lamp flies into his face and shatters on impact. Then another. He can't feel the third. A plush chair drops down on him from the hole in the ceiling without effect. A second chair dissolves before reaching him. His body swells.

"It's happening again, Nel! The stuff won't let me die! It keeps absorbing the energy used against me! For the love of Brigid, help me!" He mounts the stairs again even as the ceiling above him, along with an ornate bed, collapses toward him and quickly dissolves. Everywhere he can hear the wail of many

**27**

pleading voices: "I'm cold!" "Somebody turn me!" "Where's my grandson?" "Don't leave me like this!" "Please let me die!" among unending screams of agony and despair. Just like it was 250 years ago, Samhain remembers.

More furniture and metal kitchen implements dash through the air, all turn to sand as they near him. His body balloons further. His now tight clothes strain against his girth. "See what I've become, Nell?" Samhain screams. "We're both bloody monsters now! Help me! Help us! It's you who have the power to free us!"

Samhain reaches the upper floor. A board under him buckles but holds. "Nellie!!!" he shouts again and again.

The carnage settles. He notices specks of light, like swarms of fireflies. Their misty auras grow, radiate a cold like he'd only felt lying in the grave. "I hear you talking to me," Samhain shouts in English. "Let me help you and you help me, please? Where's Nellie Hall? Where's m' sister?"

They know. He feels them, feels their hate, for they know what he did.

"Don't you understand I wannna pay f' m' crimes? Send me to her so she can send me to hell and all of ye t' paradise."

Suddenly he knows. Through that door. Samhain nods. "Thanks."

It swings silently open. Lines of stripped metal bunk beds fill the windowless unfurnished room. Same stale smell of sweat and bodily waste. A new chill touches his soul. All around him miserable withered ashen crones materialize, some missing limbs, either naked or barely covered in rags. All turn toward him and hiss. One ragged crone drifts toward him, raising her bony arm. He feels her hate, braces for the end. Then

**28**

she stops, blinking. Her malevolence changes to wonder, then to hope.

"Sammy?" she hoarsely croaks.

He gives a Celtic hand gesture of greeting and says quietly in Irish Gaelic: "Go ahead. Kill me, Nellie. I must pay for what I did so you can fly to paradise."

Without expression she lifts her claw-like hand toward his eyes, plucks his left one out, hold it in her palm, smiles toothlessly and puts it back.

"Are you ready to kill me now?"

Her face softens, a hint of color returning to her flesh: "You're sorry. I didn't know then. I didn't believe you. I know now. It's over."

"And I must pay. Now is the time."

"No. You have paid, Sammy. I saw it. You have been to hell. So much pain. You've suffered enough. More than enough."

"But don't you remember what I did? Before I knew it was you?"

"You raped and beat me. And not just me. And you're truly sorry for every one. Each woman, somebody's sister, somebody's mother, somebody's daughter. You know that now. It's over. You know the wrongness of what you did. You were ready to pay the ultimate price. Now there's no need. I forgive you. We all forgive you."

Samhain steps back shaking his head. "Just like that? No! I must be punished and sent to hell!"

"Not to hell. Earth's not finished with you yet. Remember the books? The Annals?"

"Bloody right! You moved them after what I did to keep

**29**

them from me!"

"And now I know that was a mistake. I didn't know how sorry you were. Now I know. Now you can complete the work."

She touches his forehead with her soft pink hand. He knows. "Enniskillen! I see the exact spot!"

"You must uncover the Annals, show them to the world when it's ready. Then our people's faith and culture shall awake and live again."

"Then can I die, Nell?"

A girlish grin creases her soft face. "I can't tell you when. What's keeping you alive also keeps our Irish-Celtic culture and the hopes of grandmum alive. You're all we have left, Sammy. After all the great books are revealed to the world, when it's ready, then you can think about dying."

Slowly the other ghostly crones move toward them. Samhain recognizes some of them. They were his victims. He spins to them and falls to his knees. "I am sorry! Take your revenge on me! I'm begging you!"

Nellie turns to them. Her vibrant lips tremble. They stop. They grow youthful in seconds, smile at the two Halls and vanish forever.

Samhain blinks, amazed as his own body gradually shrinks to normal. He slowly stands up.

Nellie: "Before you ask: I just shared with them my forgiveness. Then they sensed it from you. Now they too have forgiven and are released to the next world."

"Is it really that easy?"

"It's easier in spirit. You still have far to go. You can begin by forgiving yourself."

"Easy for you to say! You expect me to feel good about what I did to you?"

"No. But I saw into your heart, I saw how you feel. How can I stay mad? Now I too can move on. You must do the same. See into your own heart. You don't have to suffer anymore. You must move on."

Samhain's face clenches for several seconds then looks up, his eyes pleading. "How do I cry? Teach me to cry."

"That will come. Happened with me after I dropped a flowerpot when I was 55. Hadn't cried since I was a baby. Cried for days. Your time will come too. Just be ready."

Samhain smiles: "You do learn fast, Nell."

"That's certain. I remember that rot you were thinking before, about the state of this place."

"Well mum always did have to pick up after you."

"Right. And you were always spotless, eh?"

"But I already was a hell-spawn."

Both of them laugh cleansing laughs.

"So, Nell, how've you been?"

"Why, I've been.... What sort of bloody question is that? How do you bloody think I've been? Dead and stuck here in England! Bloody bad fortune dying here. Now you owe me a song, brother! And you know the song!"

He chokes at the thought.

"Go to! Nobody living can hear you!"

"It's been so long, even singing to myself..."

"Well it's now or never, bub! Paradise is waiting on me. I don't intend on haunting this muck hole a minute longer!"

Samhain turns, checks left, right and behind, then stares into her beautiful face, touches her thick red hair and sings his song

**31**

for her, Sweet Nellie Hall.

The perfume of her joy fills the house. "Thank you, Samhain. I've heard the tune often, but with those bloody Greensleeves words. Even after I died, heard some muckers coming in here singing it. Dropped a couch on them, blast their eyes!"

Both laugh to their souls and embrace.

"It's time, brother. I await you in the next world."

No more words. All is complete. A final exchange of Celtic hand gestures, a smile, a warm breeze and she vanishes.


The room shakes. Blissfully, Samhain descends the stairs, floats through the heavy wooden front door as it falls off its hinges, walks out into the street, he looks back to watch the roof cave in and the brittle walls collapse inward.

Townspeople half asleep pour out of their houses and stand amazed.

"Well I'll be a bloody… They've been trying to tear that death trap down for years, now it just...."

"Hey, who are you? Were you in there?"

Samhain ignores them and keeps walking, eyes straight forward. He's found meaning for his existence. Those books! The Annals! Keep them safe, no one else left to do it. But this world's not ready yet. Christian bastards will burn them the moment they surface. Must get the people ready first. Can't die yet. When they're ready there'll be a new Ireland, England, Scotland, all the other Celtic nations united, one people and true peace.

*Mestawet Endaylalu*

♦

# My Summer Vacation Visiting Ethiopia

In the beginning of July of 2018, my daughter and I took a one-month trip to Ethiopia. The trip itself was tiresome. On top of that, waiting for the next flight for ten hours at the Frankfurt airport in Germany made that trip even more difficult. In spite of my severe leg problem, I wanted to be strong because I did not want my daughter to feel bad about the trip. This was not the first time I traveled with her to visit my birth country; it is actually my fourth time. However, this trip was different from the rest of them because I wanted my daughter to visit the place I was born in and grew up in so she could see what it looks like and observe the people.

I have lived in America for a little over twenty-five years, but going back home always makes me relive the memories of the values, culture, and norms I had while I was back home. Sometimes, I compare and contrast Ethiopia and America. Comparing these two countries makes me think about the evolution of human civilization.

My birthplace is a very small town and it is divided by even smaller villages. These villages are named by the people who have settled there, such as Qas Seffer (Priests' Village), Zebana Seffer (Security's Village), Gebeya Seffer (Market Place) and so on. The village I was born in and grew up in is called Abebe Seffer (Blossomed Village). This small town has people from

**33**

different ethnic and religious backgrounds who lived in harmony. This small town is surrounded by small and big mountains. I think because of the big mountain the name of the province is Garamuleta. The road is very difficult and during the wintertime the mountain is covered by clouds. The last three times I did not show to my daughter the exact place I was born. But this time, I decided to show her this historical place.

I have many memories about Garamuleta. Especially about my church school and the priest who taught me the Ten Commandments. He said, "We are not perfect, but in order to feel freedom in our minds, we need to try to live respecting the rules of Our Father in the Heaven." The priest's name was Yenata Gebreyes. His school was open not only for who was born Christian, but also for followers of any religion who want to learn about Christianity. My parents sent me to this church school to learn about something very important in my life. They also raised me with unconditional love that I couldn't forget through my entire life. Their love and protection made me strong. My family passed through many difficult times, but we escaped with the help of God and "God is love."

When I think of my children it is difficult for them to realize how lucky they are to be born in America. No one can understand why I am devastated by the September 11, 2011, tragedy. When I left my country, there were many tragedies that happened in my birthplace Garamuleta in the name of religion. The people who lost their lives were never involved in politics. Starting with the junta military regime, many innocent lives were taken away by a group of Islamic guerilla fighters simply because of their religion. I was raised in a Christian family and grew up surrounded by Muslims. I understand this issue deeply.

I want to tell the story of what happened to a victim of terrorism I know. She is one of the poorest women I know and her story shatters my heart whenever I remember it. The crime happened in a place called Dogu in July of 1990, three years before I left the country. She was living there with her husband and five children. Students who lived in Dogu have to go to Grawa for high school and to earn their high school diploma. These students went back to Dogo for vacation during wintertime to help their families. Thirty young male students were kidnapped by a political group named the Islamic Liberation Front. One of these students was the child of the woman I knew. This poor lady went directly to the place of these fighters. The father wanted to go but they don't like men. So, she went on the chance they would release their son due to how they have mothers too and they might feel remorseful. She stood in front of them and cried to see her son. They brought him and they slaughtered her son in front of her. Next, they slaughtered her, but they first cut her breasts to torture her. She was a dear family friend of mine. When my father learned this horrible news, he hated his life and prayed to die. In that same month, he got a stroke. My father, who I loved very dearly, died ten days later. I couldn't be there for him, the person who did so much for me. My sisters, one of my brothers and I were unable to attend our father's funeral because the guerilla fighters closed the road.

My recent journey to visit my family in Ethiopia was not easy. I was very emotional when I saw them. I lost my nephew and two of my cousins who died for unknown reasons the same year. I also lost my husband the same year. The reason I wanted to make this visit with my daughter was because I wanted her to observe the lifestyle there and gain understanding about my immigration history. Thanks God, I always appreciate being in America for many reasons.

When I went back home, I got a chance to see that poor woman's daughter in Harar. She married a Christian because she escaped from that horrible place. However, her younger brother and sister were forced to convert their religion to be a Muslim and her sister married a Muslim man. I wish to do something, but it is not easy. I gave her some Ethiopian birr, but she used part of that money to buy soft drinks and nuts for us. She made me cry because her kindness and generosity were so much like her mother's.

# Homelessness, War, Faith

"There's no place like Home." But homelessness is one of the biggest issues of this world. Homelessness is happening in every country. Even the powerful and rich countries like America. It is not easy to eliminate this problem. How can we overcome it? In order to answer this question, we need to find out the source of becoming homeless. There are many causes. The ones I will discuss are losing a job, being addicted to drugs, and being in a war zone.

Losing a job is one of the reasons that leads to being homeless in America. Some people live from paycheck to paycheck. For these people, whatever monthly pay they have goes to rent and other expenses of their life. They cannot save any money in case of emergency. When they lose their job, they lose everything, including their home. The fact is these people will most likely be placed in a shelter. Life in a shelter is not easy, and living with people from a different background from their own makes life miserable. Many of them choose to leave the shelter and prefer to live on the street.

Addiction to drugs is very bad because people who take drugs have difficulty stopping. People who are addicted use up all their money for drugs. This problem affects their entire life. Their money will never be enough for living. The more addicted they are, the sooner their life will be complicated. They will lose the energy to control their life. Worst of all, they do not only lose their homes, but their minds as well. It is a difficult life and very hard to rehabilitate. Some people who use drugs are people who have a decent amount of money. Choosing good friends is important because friends can help to cope with this bad habit. Even some families are living with these bad habits. I knew some kids whose families smoke cigarettes. The children pick up this addiction from their parents. I think everyone needs to fight against these habits because they are harmful to all human health. Instead, we should have people get into the habit of things that help their lives.

War is the most terrible and ugliest problem of this world. War cannot be over because of different people who have different ideologies. We should be able to known the difference between good and bad. For example, terrorists are killing civilians, innocent children and rescue workers. I do not think we can excuse these acts. We all have to fight to stop terrorism. Many civilians are displaced from their homes and have to leave everything behind and are forced to migrate to a safer place or to a neighboring country. Many migrants and immigrants face a hard life in a new place. In this case we can imagine how many people are made homeless.

War affects both civilians and soldiers. Some soldiers who came back from the battlefield can suffer depression and other kinds of mental disorders because of the memories of the war. Some of the soldiers may have lost friends, and they may not have a family to give them a hug when they come back home. I saw the war between Somalia and Ethiopia; it was awful. I also know about my parents' experience of war. Both of them lost their parents during the war between Italy and Ethiopia. Even at that time terrorism happened in Hararghe in the southeast part of Ethiopia. I will never forget what the terrorists did to my own family and friends living in Garamuleta, Ethiopia.

The U.S. has the best constitution in the world. Living in the USA is a great experience. Some immigrants come with the American dream. I think those people who come understanding the true history and vision, they would be successful in the USA.

The first home for everyone is the mother's womb. After birth the second home is the parents' house. When we mature, the home we need to save is the country we were born in. Our Father in Heaven gave us space on this planet. If we do not fight we can solve our problems. He creates us for good. He gave us His Words so that we can celebrate our life of good times, happiness and sadness. If we love ourselves we can love others and respect them too. If we make a mess of our lives we lose everything. The first thing we need to do is respect our parents. Our parents are also responsible for introducing us to whatever we need to know about our countries and what they learned in their lifetime. We have to respect the true history of our lives in this world that has been told from generation to the next as it was written in the Holy Bible.

*Robert Gibbons*

♦

## *the short span of night*

Her suitcase and tomato paste was borrowed from grandma,
we traveled a short span of night and there was silence;
as if someone blew out the pilot light in the old kerosene
lamp. We did not say much. Maybe there was time on our
hands. The land is beneath us. The time goes back as she
pulls into the parking lot, unlocks her back trunk. I pull
out her trunk. Some of her woman's stuff that she brings
on the trip. We both are embarrassed. Then I closed it.
Most of all I noticed it. It is just the silence that bothers me.
I could not listen to the intimacy, to be free, to be gone.

## Southern, New Jersey

I went to visit a sick relative. Had to take a bus,
do not remember the name down the center of the state.
For the bus served as a local and state service.
The deposit lives are in and out of the bus. I kept
my biggie coat close for protection from the winter chill.
As we crossed the Maurice River, it was so spoken-word.
This is the land of big shopping malls and urban sprawl.
The trees have no facial degeneration. They did not suffer
from smoke stacks or chemicals, but the roads were wide
and vacant, lots and shoppers, and super, and rotisserie,
deli, and ATM. It was faraway, but close.
The streets had names like: Liberty and Maple, Boxwood
and Captain. I could not live here.
If they expect me to buy a flatbed truck to carry dog food,
big packages are out of the question.
Pulling up to a  gas station and saying, "fill her up,"
is not in my vocal range, but I understand the innocence.

*"last night we drove through suddenly*
*warring weather, wind and lightening,*
*havoc in wires and trees."*
*(Robert Hayden)*

There is no sensation about the people left
after the storm, left ashore on Staten Island. Cut,
like guts of catfish; slice the Great Neck with knives
of Katrina and Irene. Decapitate Tallahassee roofs
to the sea with the Spanish doubloon.
The elderly strands. The names just escalate,
hurricane season or tornado alley; dust bowl
or the war of the roses. All are tricks of the light.
The predator is Mother Nature. She dissolves
the second and third floor with her acidic rain.
Crushed in the basement, safe as waste management,
left in this destruction, we raise a monument,
a hot dog stand, charge an admission fee,
put on hold our animosity, dial three-one-one,
file a missing person's report,
the whole island is on amber alert.
The trees fell through the window with its roots raised
declares kiss my ass, blasphemy or Jesus wept.

## "They buried us without shroud or coffin and in August."
### *(Seamus Heaney)*

They rushed to clear the shelves
at the community bookstore. All the titles under "H"
had been taken. So I asked the lady standing near
to review the last two, the last two copies
that were left, the last two lines. I remember
Hunter College or the Ireland House, but the shelves
were cleared of all remnants. The way the story
will be placed in the New York Times under obituary.
Maybe the academy will do a tribute, but this is not
the same Revelatory or scripted biography
when the book captures a famous life. The shelves
were cleared, left to rest in place of many names;
the way Dickinson used her numbers
or Shakespeare used sonnets. The way we forget
he was Irish and I am English. The way we forget
after the shelves are cleared and the food taken
that longevity has the potential to sustain.

I did not come to pay respect. The way window sills
and shelves are placed at school, but we are warned
of this, asked the dust of boards and then sit and wait
for the inevitable, for the perpetual and listen to the
rain spit into new ashes. For we asked to see before

**43**

sight and live before life and not show and tell, but
there are loads of dust and lots of ashes to remain here.

If there is not a return then why is the passport green
and a return back to the old country; to a place
of imagination so that the artificial will cease.
If the course is anointed with voice and muse,
only if I arrived to those shelves before goose wings
had taken them, left to the void. The clearing
of the shelves, left, only another glory, another story
to create from threadbare necessity,
only left the rest to wait.

## *Transtomer*

I saw ghost in the third grade discovering the passing
of my great-grandmother. She spoke to me the night
before telling me she is leaving. She speaks to me
of her transition. It becomes an obsession, these
ancestor voices, could not accept them as gifts for
fear of psychosis. My dreams are more than mere
dream. It is lifting trance. It is lifting out of the
physical world. When this double speak tells me
things. I have been selected to be a portal for a
people. This double speak tells me not to be afraid
of the future. There, at the graveside cleaning
the plots of an ancestor looking for the answer
to this composition is constant decomposition.
It erodes into a death notebook.

One night, a large window opens in the suburb
of Queens. There among the large trees were
people in manumission. All kinds of people mostly
women flying into the sky. Whose people were they?
Where were they going? They were flying down
from sky. They were speaking but I could not discern
their words. It is inaudible these people. Could not
recognize their faces, crowds of someone's people
coming down from a large tree in Queens.
They wore gowns and uniforms. They moved in crowds.
These people that stopped by my square window

with my view of the large tree in the suburb of Queens.
Where were they going in this dark nothingness? In this
suburb of Queens, in this realm of fantasy,
but it is real and it still comes back when it wants.
It haunts me and it taunts me, these people flying
through the suburbs of Queens. I am still
a ward of this state. I am in dream between worlds.

# *a peace lily on a compost heap*

the world is rosewater, there you are
in this receptacle full of metaphor
the colors of rhubarb and blood-orange
sangria; the time I tried to raise you
out front and decided it too much
sun and damp wetness, the manicure
of hair follicles between teeth, the relief
of fifteen orgasms, the filthy and sloppy
of plowing in deep earth, the fertility
is to crave birth and I want to create
want to plow until irrigation is not
enough, the flood in the heart-shaped
lake, the Katsura and London plane
hang low in this botanic garden
this is so natural as symbiosis happens
want peace for there is no repose
and this is not a proposal, but moaning
flesh, a litmus test of soil and not sure
of the harvest, not sure who make it
the farthest.

## *Antioch, Tennessee*

you may call it prayer because my mother is here,
but the roads are slick and lonely where the bare cold
rolls down this neighborhood. There are no birds, just
earthworms sizzle on fresh concrete in the bottom
of a skillet as I search for verse in this overworked ground

full of dull yellow and black bottom brown; people mind
their business and I guess I should leave the rest to history.
The news of the day is that it is snowing in Memphis, so
there is no reason to be restless. I am still blessed with
family, monogamy of blood. They have come here for one
for the first time on holiday.

For a solitary function to be together and I thought I would
enjoy central time. I want Florida like the dragonfly. The
migration down South but the word of mouth for a few
more days in the old year. Just a few more days for salvation.
It can't be saved by church or synagogue, but the dialogue
of nephews and nieces and pieces of potato pie. Giblets

of collard green made with love and the stove still steams
in my background. I will leave in a few days in the old year,
new and few memories, will leave the old year behind, then
I can find my way back through the calendar. It will be the
rush of trucks and the run of the expressway. This is enough
to frame my thoughts, enough to say have gained memory
only one moment.

# Sanford, Florida

At first, I did not think I needed to write a poem
because so much has been written for fear
of exposure, but I have lived in the sun all my life.
I will not get sun-burned. The melanin protects me
like my grandmother's ice cream churn and we
do not burn in Florida. Only the lard and grease
of a spider's skillet when we heard the news.
The many electrocuted on the chair, but I am Floridian.
The home of blue herons and egrets, mallards
and alligators. The skin toughens like sawgrass.
The sun goes down in half-mast, late in the evening.
The pending heat stroke will creep like a chameleon.

I am a Floridian. I know what happens when the heat
will make anger rise from cesspool green,
ripe mango-avocado, sugarcane with the cud to spit out,
left to deteriorate. I know where you are on this,
on the other side of the state. You will probably
take advantage culture capitalize but will not
live next to me. I call you out with your systemic
and endemic, beyond the evidence.

This is the reason I smelled something rotten
in Apopka, Florida. My grandfather told me,
we are not going to that end of town. It does not matter
about statistics, quotes, and picture flashes.
We are referring to Jackie Robinson.
It is better to leave town. I will never convince,

will not fear the sun. The brutal tailgate of a gator.
The exotic temperature is annual, pander the bottom
of the state like an invasion of pythons.
I am natural, not colored by the sun, but protected
and resurrected from the swamp of folktale.

*Marlene Glasser*

◆

# *Two Creeps*

I hated my nurse shoes. My father made me get them. He felt I was growing fast and needed supportive shoes for my high arches. Or, maybe, he was too cheap to buy me those fashionable loafers I so much wanted. All my friends had Buster Brown saddle shoes in two tones, either darker brown and white, or black and white, which I coveted.

My small heart feared and loathed the prospect of returning to school in the fall, because everyone would see me wearing those horrible nurse shoes, with a steel shank for extra support. They must have been made of iron or at least stainless steel, because they were indestructible. Believe me I tried my hardest to destroy them. I threw them down several flights of stairs without me in them, to avoid trauma to myself. When I got to the bottom of the stairs they didn't have a dent in them.

I also tried drowning them in a bathtub. Unfortunately, they were still serviceable. When my mother noticed that they were wet, she just put them on the clothesline with the wash. They were pinned up with wooden clothespins and flapping in the wind for all my neighbors to see my shame and humiliation. I could swear they smiled at me as I walked by them cursing.

In the fall, I planned to step in every puddle of muddy water if they were still alive. If that didn't work there were always snow and hailstorms to count on to wear them down. I began to

**51**

plan my attack in bed at night. I thought of stealing my brother's Swiss army knife and using it to mutilate my nemesis. A few scratches and my parents would never notice. But over time the imperfections would mount up and eventually cause their demise.

My mother noticed my brother's knife concealed in my pillowcase one day. While she was doing the wash she returned it to his top drawer. I could steal it again, but I didn't know if she would catch me, and if she did, there would be hell to pay. So I just kept quiet, just like she did. Perhaps my mother foolishly thought I would forget about the matter in time.

However, she was under a silly misconception if she believed that. I think my mom didn't remember how important it is to look good in front of your peers.

I had an important mission to accomplish before school started. No one was going to get in my way, not my brother, my mother, or even my father. By this time, I was thinking of adding my father to the hit list. As it was getting closer to September, I was becoming more and more anxious and worried about my future at my elementary school. I was concerned about becoming a laughing stock because of my nurse shoes. Probably, I wouldn't have any friends left. Or I might be demoted from the popular group of kids to the nerdy kids. I didn't know any of the nerdy kids. And I didn't want to meet any of those pimply little jerks anyway.

I hoped my mother wouldn't notice that I kept my fork after dinner. I thought I could pierce a few small holes and scratch the Hades out of them. However, my father fooled me. When I went to sleep and put my shoes down at the foot of my bed, instead of in my closet Friday night, my father stole them and secretly polished them to perfection. Those two creeps looked even better than when they were new, my dad had polished them to such a high gloss. I could even see my reflection in them. This was a terrible shock for an eight-year-old to wake up to early on a Saturday morning.

Time was running out. I had to really think hard about how to execute those creeps. I think a major part of my problem was that I had a pair of devious parents. They apparently couldn't be trusted. They seemed to relish every opportunity to foil my great efforts at destroying these heinous shoes. I had to be sneakier than them. I hated to stoop to my parents' level, but I had no choice.

I decided to bring in reinforcements and let my best friend, Judy, know about my problem, and ask her to help me. So I showed her a picture of the horrible pair in a nursing catalogue. I found it hidden amongst my father's Playboy magazines. I couldn't bear to let her see me in my nurse shoes. I hoped my father wasn't getting me a new pair for next year. What a disaster! I couldn't worry about that. I had to worry about this year's model first.

I went for a sleepover at Judy's house that weekend. This gave me plenty of time for consultation and action. Judy had a dog. A big fat mean black dog. My mind began racing with excitement with all of the scenarios that could happen at Judy's with Sammy, her dog. If I bring those two creeps along with me, I thought, maybe something could be arranged. Possibly a kidnapping. Conceivably I could put something of interest to Sammy in them, like a raw steak. Sammy might accidentally tear them apart while enjoying his steak dinner. He might decide to bury them under a bush in Judy's backyard, or even dig a hole near his dog house so that he could play with them at his leisure. He might take them into his dog house for a visit of biting and chewing. I smirked, "Oh Sammy, I love your big mean face."

The beauty of this little escapade was that I wouldn't get blamed and my parents might never find them. My folks might even get me a new pairs of shoes of my own choosing, because they were stolen by a big evil dog. They would feel so sorry for me that I would never see a pair of white nurse shoes again. If that didn't work, there was always Judy to plot with.

I prepared for the final reckoning with the Two Creeps. Emptying my piggybank named Fatso all over my bedroom carpet revealed I had $23.97. Anticipating total victory, I promised Sammy I would rename Fatso after him in honor of his great destruction. And it felt good, really good, I mean fantastic! The butcher provided me with two prime cuts of filet mignon dripping with scarlet blood.

As soon as I got to Judy's house I ran straight for the refrigerator and placed the twin beauties in the very, very back of the third shelf between the artichoke salad and rice pudding. For luck I took a few spoonfuls of rice pudding. On the eve of destruction, I placed those steaks into the two creeps and swatted them both goodbye.

Sammy gleefully approached the horrible pair and devoured the steaks alarmingly fast. Blood sped its way to the walls of Judy's bedroom as Sammy violently continued to bite beyond the meat and into the flesh of the two monsters. His massive teeth were stronger than double steel saw blades. The two were finally a mess of shredded pulp, scattered all over Judy's bedroom. Sammy wore a satisfied snicker a mile wide.

I laughed and laughed so hard, I began to cry. With that I rolled around the carpet with Sammy petting and laughing some more. The terrible two were no more. They had been completely torn apart by the merry beast. Their remains were completely scattered around Judy's bedroom, the walls of which were caked in scarlet sticky blood and the whites of leather from my nurse shoes. It was so satisfying that I took multiple pictures of the carnage to show to my parents and all of the kids at school. Judy and I smiled as we looked through the new Buster Brown catalog and I picked out the shoes I wanted.

My sneaky parents could hardly object to purchasing a new pair of Buster Browns now that I didn't have any shoes left. I started spontaneously practicing crying to emphasize how bad I was feeling. I practiced feeling stressed and upset about the loss of the two creeps so that I could be fully prepared for making a tearful phone call to my parents to explain the situation.

When I called my parents crying I was so impressive that I think even my parents were a bit in shock. I truly deserved an Academy Award for the best child performance in the major picture of life. Afterwards, the three of us engaged in a victory dance. Sammy stood up on his hind legs still fresh with blood all over his body. We didn't mind that the blood got all over our bodies. I actually found it comforting and oh so freeing. I had already composed a triumph theme song to the melody of "Shake, Rattle and Roll." Judy got out her harmonica and I improvised with my kazoo. We danced and screamed to the song gleefully as Sammy surprisingly barked along in tune until we all fell onto Judy's bed in exhaustion. Then Judy and I gave each other many, many high fives.

Sammy committed a wonderful crime. He was truly my savior and my new love. I kissed his bloody face, chest and paws in homage and deep respect. The eradication of the terrible two was a bloodthirsty triumph of master planning and precise execution in which my parents would never suspect my involvement.

Judy and I bowed our heads, crossed ourselves, and kneeled on our knees in gratitude, entering into a brief prayer to God. We needed to acknowledge this magical transgressive, tremendously satisfying moment which wouldn't be possible without the aid and guidance of our Lord Mother. I realized we had acted in concert a lot like the Holy Trinity, and that made my little heart oh so happy.

*George Holmes*

♦

# Humphrey and the Foie Gras

He sat next to me in class when we were 11, after passing the fatal 11 Plus exam in my UK school. The exam separated the sheep from the goats. Humphrey was a large boy. There seemed to be lots of him when he stood up and when he sat down, spreading out amoeba-like, bag on one side, gloves, scarf, hat on the other, spilling out sandwiches which his devoted mother always prepared for him though how she got the cash for some of those sandwich ingredients was anyone's guess. From his capacious bag spilled papers, pencils, boxes of insects and wild flowers. His bag, red in color, had a dragon painted on it. "So Humphrey can find it easily," his mother confided to me one day. She rather took to me. "Gerald," she said, "Humphrey is a good boy. And so are you."

I didn't call him Humphrey. I called him Harrison! We all called ourselves by our surnames, as did our school masters. So he was H.H. I was G. H., therefore just before him in morning attendance call when we paid our four pennies for the school dinner, except Humphrey and I were "free" students. We just said "free" and the teacher moved on, counting pennies, six-pences, shillings, ha'pennies, even farthings from the other boys. No one said anything about us being free but it meant that our mums had not the wherewithal to pay. So when Humphrey shared his foie gras sandwich with me and I told my mum she said, "Where does she get the money for that, I wonder?" and obviously she told Mrs. Vogel and Mrs. Lannet who clucked their tongues.

Mrs. Harrison was a pretty woman. Her husband was in the war but she seemed to have admirers and was often down the pub, the Jolly Minstrels. I know that because Harrison and I had to sit in the garden and deal with lemonades and bags of crisps while our mums lived it up in the saloon bar with Sid and Harold, always good for a laugh, Mum said. She also said I was not to say anything to my teachers about going to the pub but the teachers used to go, too. When I pointed that out, she said, "Oh, shush…."

It turned out that Mrs. Humphrey worked at Anzani, a local factory where she was in charge of a machine that made ploughs which became popular since we all had to grow vegetables instead of flowers in our gardens and people who could afford them bought little ploughs and grew huge marrows and runner beans. Mr Lamton who owned the factory used to give her these special sandwich ingredients as he knew someone who knew someone who had connections and his son was in the same regiment as Mr. Humphrey. So he had a soft spot for Mrs. H and hence the foie gras. Mum sniffed when she heard that but then she went to the pub, too, and when she came home after at least two port and lemons and bearing two pairs of nylons from Mr. Lambert who gave me a shilling one day and said "Mum's the word eh, Gerald?" she could not really complain. Rules had to be bent in the war didn't they? Ways and means. Make do and mend. How to make a meat pie without meat. It was the little perks that kept us going, a pair of nylons here, some foie gras there. People who knew someone who knew someone. Mum's the word because loose lips sink ships.

So that is how I had foie gras sandwiches during the war. Humphrey and I remained friends and I supported him when he ran for the city council. There were always ways and means. We profited from the lessons learned during the war.

# Iron Bars

After perusing the crowded shelves of the health food shop, I finally asked for assistance: "Do you have those iron bars? Nutrition bars I mean, with iron? I've been told I'm anemic and need iron." I had drifted in to the shop as it was raining.

A rather grandly dressed young man peered down at me from the length of his rather prominent patrician nose.

"Yes, we do," he said. "Now there are three types, 100% iron which is $40.00 for 30 tablets. Take two a day. We recommend a course of three months. This could be dangerous if you're pregnant or expect to be." He paused.

Smiling enigmatically I said, "Maybe I should hear about the alternatives."

"Well," he said, "there's slim line iron 50%, $65.00 for the same amount but it includes the finest of vitamins in a luxury bed of Belgian chocolate, soy and whole grain oats, worried at the mill but not crushed." He looked at me critically. I pulled in my stomach.

"And the last one?"

"That's for women with glandular problems, Madam, who need iron but it does have some side effects such as hebetude and inability to concentrate over a long period."

(I vowed to look up hebetude when I got in as I would have liked to take him down a peg or two but kept quiet. Best to be sure of one's ground with snootiness).

"Those are $55.00 for a week's supply."

A man hovering nearby said: "You looking for iron, lady?"

"Yes," I replied.

"Well," he said, "take those iodine tablets with iron. The wife did and she's right as rain now. No stopping her."

"Thanks," I said, "how much?"

"$4.00 for a hundred. Get them at CVS."

"Thank you, I will."

The snooty young man drifted away. He knew he'd sell some of his pills that day. A woman with a helpless look and too much lipstick was already approaching him.

# Dog

"Did you write it down?" said Isabel his therapist. Bert nodded.

"Yes, I did, just like you told me to. I have a pad and pen ready at the bedside and have trained myself to note the facts and ideas of my dreams. It works. Otherwise I quickly forget them.

"In this dream I was at home looking through the advertisements in a paper or magazine and caught sight of one reading: *Good dog looking for new home. A friend.* I thought it curious. I am a lonely sort of person and always wanted a friend and had thought of getting another cat after Gertie left for a good home during the time I was touring in musicals. Cats can be inscrutable and not really companionable. And so there it was: a dog. I knew I'd have to walk a dog regularly and give it shots. All this went through my mind in a twinkling of the dream. I recalled that all dogs are ninety-eight per cent wolves, even those awful looking Chihuahuas. What people see in naked dogs I don't know, but there's no accounting for taste except of course a lot of people don't have any. Don't get me started."

"Are we still in the dream?" queried Isabel

"Oh yes, sorry. I called the number in the advertisement and after several rings, a sharp voiced female said, *Yes, who is it? If you're from the Democrats or Meals on Wheels, let me remind you that we're in a recession. Well, speak up. You're not a heavy breather are you?*

*No, I've called about the dog.*

*The dog? Oh you mean the friend?*

*Yes, the friend. Is he for sale?*

*Oh, we're not selling him. We're giving him away."*

*Why is that?*

*Why? That's our business. Are you single?*

"I was somewhat taken aback by that abrupt change of question, Isabel. I blurted out that I was."

"Which is true," said Isabel.

Bert continued:

"I said to the woman, *What's that have to do with it?*

*Oh, nothing,* she said. *My name's Irene. Do you want to come round to see our friend? His name's Alexander. How about tonight, six pm do you ok? Come for a drink. You do drink don't you? Alex likes a merry person.*

*Why are you giving him away,* I asked again.

*Well, it's mother. She's allergic to fur. You're not furry are you? Hirsute?*

I stammered that I was somewhat. Well, a lot really.

*Oh,* she said. *Maybe you could shave before this evening or maybe just wear a tie or better still a turtleneck. Then mother wouldn't know. Are your hands furry? Think of gloves. Suede. See you around 6 as arranged. Here's the address. We'll let Alex sniff you to see if you pass muster."*

Bert looked at Isabel who asked him what he thought it meant. "Well, I was concerned that there might not be a dog at all. Irene was very pushy on the phone. I don't like pushy women."

"Do you know any?" asked Isabel.

"Well no, well yes, first of all: that bitch at work, Veronica. Oh, I shouldn't have said that but she's so demanding. I was joking around with Sybil the other day, Sybil's desk is next to mine, telling her I was swimming in plastic bags as they give you so many in the shops and Veronica was passing and said didn't I know that if one placed all the plastic bags end to end, (as if one would), they would go to and from the moon several times because they were not bio-degradable and she called me an anti-ecologian. That was her word. Sybil had of course taken herself to the ladies during Veronica's harangue. Well, she needs the job because her mother has to have special medication being allergic to fur. Oh my God, that dream! It has a basis in reality. I've got to ask her if she has a dog, privately of course, when Veronica is not around. And now I think of it, I came in the office the other day and caught Sybil looking at what I think was a porn site featuring hairy men. I coughed and said I had just come in. It's like life is a part of that dream. I hope I don't dream any more as I suspect, Isabel, that Sybil has got a sort of yen for me what with my hairy chest and all. One hot day in summer I wore an open necked shirt and caught Sybil looking hard and long at my chest, as I have to trim my fur."

"Oh," said Isabel. "We're at the end of today's session. You're breaking through the dream barrier. See you next time."

Bert had a late meal and went to bed. His dream came quickly in that REM period so much in the news recently. He was on a bus on the way to see Irene and Alexander and the fur allergic mother Claudia though how he knew her name was not clear. The house was set back from the road and surrounded by thick bushes of a sort he's not seen before, giving off a peculiar odor. He rang the bell. The door opened quickly and dream Irene or was it office Sybil or even therapist Isabel opened the door. He heard a dog bark.

*Hello,* she said, *I'm Irene. Come in. Alexander is in the lounge where he sleeps. Come in for a sniff and what about a snifter? Ha ha ha!*

Bert followed her in. *Don't worry about mother. I've locked her in her room with plenty of water. She likes water. It's good for you.*

Suddenly paralyzed, unable to speak he lifted one arm which held a long gleaming glittering knife and drove it hard against the neck of dream Irene or was it Isabel or Sybil or bitch Veronica?

When they found him two days later after repeated calls to his home were not answered, he was dead of a massive aneurysm, his blood splattered over the carpet. The puzzling thing was he had a dog leash in his hand that could not be dislodged from his grip. Isabel was called to the inquest but said nothing of the dreams. She was one for patient confidentiality. Bert's sister from LA found some scrappy notes about dreams but burnt them. The leash was never explained.

*Audrey Israele*

♦

## *My Lesson Plans*

When I started teaching we got a new principal and she held a meeting in which she said she wanted us to hand in lesson plans every Monday morning for the entire week. I didn't like writing lessons plans. I liked to work spontaneously, but she insisted that we hand them in. I did it for a while. But I believed she wasn't really reading them, so I decided to trick her.

I had first grade that year so I wrote some crazy plans:

Monday
>9 a.m. Discuss Einstein's Theory of Relativity
>11 a.m. Snack time
>1 p.m. Freud's theory of the ego and the id
>2 p.m. Physics
Tuesday
>9 a.m. Read *Hamlet*
>11 a.m. Snack
>1 p.m. Trigonometry
>2 p.m. Calculus
Wednesday
>9 a.m. Study French
>11 a.m. Snack
>1 p.m. Chemistry Lab
>2 p.m. Algebra

Thursday
9 a.m. Discuss the American Revolution.
11 a.m. Snack
1 p.m. Read *Paradise Lost*
2 p.m. The inventions of Thomas Edison
Friday
9 a.m. Read *A Tale of Two Cities.*
11 a.m. Snack
1 p.m. Listen to Vivaldi's the *Four Seasons.*
2 p.m. Write an autobiography. Read and talk about grammatical errors.

I handed this in. The principal gave it back to me at 3 o'clock with her initials and an "OK" on the bottom. She obviously hadn't read it.

I should have kept my mouth shut, but I said to her, "Read it again." So she did and was very embarrassed. My effort backfired because from then on she read every word of my plans for the rest of the year.

Me and my big mouth.

P.S. The principal left after one year and never came back.

*Angela Kingland*

♦

## *Climate Change*

Disgusting garbage, poisoned air, deadly chemicals, polluted lakes, rivers, streams, beaches and waterways are only the tip of the iceberg. The destruction of trees, plants, birds, insects, sea creatures, animals and reptiles, are all a significant part of what is now known to be contributing to climate change. Oil pollution is another big problem and so are coalmines. The warming of the air leading to the melting of the ice glaciers that are flooding the ocean is the cause of shrinking land. The earth is rapidly changing and we are doing it by our behavior, lifestyle, ignorance, actions, lack of knowledge and denial. Environmental emission trackers in New Zealand show what is taking place. Oxygen and nitrogen are decreasing while the amounts of greenhouse gasses like carbon dioxide and methane are increasing.

Climate change is real and we need to do our part to stop this disaster that is coming; time is of the essence. Our Earth is the most precious piece of real estate given to us by Him. There are so many destructive forces on the earth like ISIS, jihad, Islamic militants, K.K.K., White supremacists, and other groups. War is already killing people and the environment. Education is needed—the knowledge of what helps to prevent climate change and how to survive on this Earth. However, by not doing our part extinction on this Earth will come and we will be doomed. There has to be more we can do to appreciate and learn about our Earth. Are we trying to make history for the Guinness Book of Records?

There are those of you who say that's nonsense, that this Earth is always going to be here, it is not going anywhere, and I can throw my stuff where the hell I want, all that shit does not interest me. Remember this, fracking can cause tremors and make a substantial amount of wastewater. Although crude and natural oils are produced, it can be dangerous to the very water and food we use. If your tap water is polluted with radium, benzene, and other toxins, would you be able to use it? The federal and state governments have already reaped over $60 billion from fracking. People have become billionaires by selling their land to companies for fracking. Now, do you think any law is going to come about for safety requirements?

So get up and smell the coffee; take action now. Climate change is here. Let us save the Earth and stop being naïve. Appreciation for our Earth starts now. Think of the Philippines experiencing the tsunami, the close call with Japan's Fukushima nuclear leaks. Canada, Germany, and India to name a few had their share of near misses. Disaster in Russia's Chernobyl was another wake up call. We do not need a nuclear world, only a safe one. Earthquakes, storms, landslides, hurricanes, and tornadoes will always affect us. But with climate change and our irresponsible behavior the worst is yet to come.

America was taken out from the climate agreement with other countries, yet we are number two in polluting the world; only China is worse. Let us stop climate change and save our Earth, lives, and health. Is it too much to put our garbage in the appropriate bins instead of the trains, busses, bushes and streets? Stop the use of plastic that is filling the world. Hold people accountable for dumping garbage. Encouragement, example, and consequence will bring change. Then people will look and listen and hopefully sooner than later a clean environment will appear. Toxic air contributes to the cause of cancer, sinus problems, asthma, allergy, heart disease and other medical issues that are deadly. Look at the big picture of what we are doing to the Earth. Our water and food must not be polluted because this will cause disease. Poachers are killing the wild animals for gain. These animals must be on this Earth with us. The trafficking of wild animals and people concerns me greatly.

Trees help protect us from carbon dioxide poison. Cutting down trees means there is nothing to hold the soil together. This weakens the earth and causes mudslides. Many people are killed too often due to trees that are gone. When there is not anything to hold the soil firm the earth comes collapsing— then homes and people. Please leave the trees unless there is a necessity to cut them. They have a purpose.

The grass is no longer greener on either side.

I applauded the people who are on the path to saving the Earth, its environment and inhabitants, like in my country of birth. In Trinidad and Tobago, the leatherback turtles are no longer extinct thanks to a woman named Susan and her team. People need to realize with every unintelligent action, such as leaving food and garbage on the beach, there is a reaction. Our precious treasure that was put here for us is not to be abused or taken for granted but to be appreciated and enjoyed. All it takes is smart living and practicing to do the right thing. Even the Pope sees the need for change to save the Earth, so isn't that telling us something about our ignorance? Well, if it speaks to you then join the club and let us do what is right now not later when the ocean has taken over the land and life for everyone and everything is extinct.

If water does takes over what would we live on? On boats on lakes, oceans, the Amazon River? Terra firma is better.

Look up and see the rising or setting of the bright beautiful splendor of the sun or the brilliant glittering of stars and moon. The falling of warm rain or ice drops can be delightful. Glorious white snow and intricately formed ice like crystal diamonds are most incredible beauties. Rainbow colors look like colored candy across the sky. Here is a picture of elegance on a runway of blue, gray and white clouds. We have trees with leaves that change their shade to red, yellow, gold, orange, pink, crimson, lighter shades of green and brown, like a child's dream. Precious are the land and the trees, vines and bushes with fruit and vegetables to feed any hungry belly in dramatic colors and textures.

Now, all that is threatened we need to take care of. So tell me you do not care. Stop making stories you do not believe it, there is no such thing you say. Why are there so many floods, storms, fires, clogged waterways all across the Earth? You are seeing what I am seeing so do not wait, come on board, let us work as a united front to save our Earth, please people. Something must be done to prevent polluted air and for safe water, food, and life. Better health with fewer new diseases. We need laws on shale fracking, for healthy people and a clean environment. I can't preach. Writing is easier and I think more effective to bring changes, so let's sing the same song: save our Earth. Save it! Save it!

# A Home is Haunted

She was hearing them for sure. Only last year they had bought
the house. Not even a year—just seven months. It was October.
Last night Mama Arleen's daughter June woke at exactly mid-
night screaming her head off, calling "Mama, Mama, there are
people in the room." Mama Arleen went in, turned the light on,
held her close. June was so scared and could not stop crying
because she was afraid of the dark, too.

Mama Arleen stayed with her calming her down and finally
she went back to sleep. As Mama Arleen returned to bed about
15 minutes later she heard them: "Get out, get out of here!" Exactly what June said she had heard. Mama Arleen sat up. Again
and again she heard, "Get out, get out and go; you do not belong here, go leave!" Then all was quiet after Mama Arleen
started saying the Hail Mary over and over until she went into a
deep sleep. Three hours later she was awakened by laughter.
"Haha, Haha." With her husband out of town, Mama Arleen
was really darned scared and shaken. It got worse: "Heeee,
haaa, heee, haaaa, wooo, wooo, haaaa, haaaaa."

Mama Arleen thought, oh, my God, this house is haunted.
She got on her knees as if she was back in the convent with the
nuns. She started to pray the Lord's Prayer, then the "Lord is
my shepherd." When she rose she heard, "Haaah, heee, heee,
haaah, heee, haaaah, heeeeee. It will not help!" At this moment
Mama Arleen became frantic. Then, at 7 a.m. June started to
call, "Are you there Mama?" She answered, "Honey it's alright,
I am coming." She went to her daughter and sat on the bed
holding her. June asked, "Who were those people talking last

night?" She said, "Oh, honey, I do not know but I will take care of everything." June replied, "But, Mama, they said, get out, go leave, you do not belong here. Mama, I am sacred. I do not want to stay here." Mama Arleen said, "But, honey, we can't just leave when a problem comes and your Dad is out of town. He has to be told about this when he returns."

They had their breakfast. Then June left for school while Mama Arleen went to work. All day, Mama Arleen thought she should discuss the issue with a nun from her convent, and finally she went to see Mother Rita. Mother Rita promised to bring a prayer group to the new home to get those spirits who were entering the haunted house. She said I know all about these things and with faith and prayer the invaders will leave.

Dad Andy came home the following day and, with no time wasted, June ran to her dad to inform him of her ordeal with the unseen visitors. She was crying and insisted they move away from the scary home. She said, "Dad, I miss you, please, please do not leave us here alone." June said, "We can't stay here, we must leave, we must get out and go." Mama Arleen said to Andy, "There were voices coming from the attic and it was frightening and we were worried. But now that you are here we can take care of this issue."

Minutes later when assured that Dad would solve the problem, June went to her room giving Dad and Mom time to talk. Andy asked his wife to set up a meeting with Mother Rita on Friday the 13th. June was to be at her grandma's for the weekend. The prayer group would arrive at 9 p.m. Mother Rita came with seven others. She brought holy water, incense, black candles, a rosary, olive oil, garlic, and white candles. They went up to the attic and sat in a circle while Mother Rita started to read the 23rd Psalm. She went Psalm after Psalm telling the evil spirits to leave. She anointed everyone with the olive oil and holy water on their faces and hands. She then took out a small bottle of blessed salt from her pocket and went to each corner sprinkling the salt. They sang many hymns calling on the evil spirits to depart.

Mother Rita shouted, "In the name of Jesus I command you evil spirits to leave." She repeated this at least three times. They all felt a cool breeze filling the attic. "Thank, God," said Mother Rita. She then lit a black candle and placed three white ones around it. All of sudden, the black candle went out. The group then started to sing, "Our Father." Mama Arleen and Papa Andy had a feeling of peace and spirituality and knew things would be fine now. When Mother Rita was leaving with the prayer group later that night she told the parents to keep the Bible opened to Psalm 23.

The next day, June said to her parents I slept all night and am not scared anymore. Her parents looked at her and said the spirits left and will not be back ever. June had time with them reading and playing games throughout the day. She suddenly asked her Mama, "Do dead people come visiting only for Halloween?" Mama Arleen said, "Sometimes, honey, if they can and are restless." June said, "So is that why the people were here and were upset that we were in the house? Well, next Halloween we will spend it by Grandma and let them have their peace and love together as a family." Mama Arleen answered, "Oh, June that's a great idea, isn't it Dad? Thank you, June, for helping to bring tranquility to fill this home." June said, "Now we don't have to move ever."

# What Matters?

Everything matters to me while I am alive on earth and functioning. Being interested in what is around me is important to my family; my birth country, Trinidad and Tobago; also my adopted country, the United States of America; the Earth and its inhabitants; and to God. The things I do and say in my life can affect others across the world. I must always think of those who are being killed, raped, kidnapped, mentally and physically abused, enslaved. Those who suffer from hunger and thirst. All the forgotten victims, both human and animal. Many people have lost their lives trying to escape oppression, famine and war. Mothers are still stranded outside fenced off countries. Families lack homes and basic necessities, medical help and support. People are locked up due to lack of money, lies, corruption, false witness. I cannot pretend and act naïve that all these things do not happen. I am not in a fool's paradise; I know there are wicked killers like ISIS and the Hutus. I must support those who stand up for the baggage carriers, the human rights victims, for those people who need to leave their homes running, walking, sailing in dangerous boats, riding unsafe vehicles and becoming prey to pirates who steal what little they have while sometimes also raping them and causing their death.

The rich and powerful, the ignorant and arrogant, the selfish and greedy are the ones ignoring the poor, homeless, hopeless, powerless and voiceless. These people are of any race, color, class, creed, sex, religion. These are the people in the positon to uphold law and order, but tend to be corrupt, com-

**74**

passionless, envious, and wicked. True, there are the missionaries, the United Nations, human rights workers, emergency and medical personnel, servicemen and women, and world leaders who do what it takes to genuinely bring peace, protection and safety around the world. On the other hand, too often leaders kill and jail protestors who speak out and refuse to support their wicked ways. Leading for them is not about the country; only about the power and the money. They build and compile nuclear weapons to use on other nations and chemical weapons to use on their own citizens. These leaders order the killing of religious, ethnic, and racial minorities that result in genocide. They murder their own people, start civil wars, and do not step down even after being voted out. These leaders want to remain in power forever and ever. They are hindrances to the entire world.

It matters that they get away with the evil they do. What matters are those with the strength, stamina, willpower, time, knowledge, and patience to help save these many troubled, problematic nations. It is hard to believe the world will ever come together in a unified matter. Still, the Almighty can make this world a safer and better place to live, as can human generosity, hospitality, patience, commitment, care and love for others who are in pain and suffering. Right now is the time to help the refugees, immigrants and migrants, asylum seekers, the wandering and the lost. Time is of the essence in getting people the help they need. It matters that enough is not yet being done.

## What I Dare to Dream

To dream of conquering good over evil.

To dream that love will fill the world uniting all the people.

To dream of equality for all regardless of color, race, religion or sex.

To dream of protecting the mentally and physically challenged, seniors, the helpless and the innocent from sexual abusers.

To dream of people living in peace throughout the world.

To dream of stopping the violence and evil throughout the world.

To dream of sheltering the homeless and unfortunate.

To dream of freedom for people of all nations, big or small.

To dream of world leaders talking to solve problems instead of wars and sanctions.

To dream of ending childhood diseases.

To dream of educating children around the world for their own safety and knowledge.

To dream of ending sexual exploitation throughout the world.

To dream of respecting people's sexual preferences.

To dream of eradicating world hunger and thirst.

To dream of protecting the world from illicit drugs.

To dream of saving the environment and its inhabitants from poachers.

To dream of helping all persons become productive human beings.

To dream of keeping guns out of the hands of people who should not be armed.

And to dream of preventing world leaders from building and using nuclear weapons.

These are my dreams. What do you dare to dream?

♦

# *Longing*

Ella Louise Gray had been brought up rich and privileged all her life, her father being one of the only two doctors in Cedars Grove, and her mother, a rich debutant, coming from very old money. All her friends were always boasting about how much money they had or their latest shopping sprees, vacation or whatnot. Which bored Ella to tears. She felt as if she had been born too soon, or in another time. And she felt as if she did not belong here. She did not know if it was growing pains or if there was something more, to what was going on, in her head; after all, she was only ten years old. Ella felt like it was her destiny to be and to do something more with her life. Or at least when she grew older.

Ella always felt sad, when her father, Sir Robert Gray, sometimes took her in their motorized car, to see some of his patients on the other side of town. It pained her to see children her age or younger living in such poverty, with old, worn out, frayed, discolored clothes, and it was then and there she decided that she was going to help do something about it. So she asked her father how could this be when they had so much; his answer did not satisfy Ella's thirst for knowledge. So she told him that she was going to do her part or at least try and change this situation. So she told her mother, relatives and friends about her discovery and if ever they had any leftover food, canned goods, used clothing, shoes, new or worn, toys and books, anything they did not need she would take them. Her dad was a bit apprehensive, but her mother was very adamant about it, and said no out right. Then father spoke to mother and she caved in.

Sadly, many of her so-called friends and her two cousins, Mary Lou and Pembroke, laughed and thought that she should not be fraternizing with the other side of Cedars Grove. And that they were too high-class to be even thinking of helping those less fortunate than themselves. But she knew then and there even at ten years old, that she Ella Louise Gray, was put on this earth to do more than just be rich and privileged.

# Her Family

Sometimes I wonder if I was switched at birth or stolen from the hospital and given to my oh so strange and creepy family. I mean they love me, this I know, but from zero until the age of ten which I am now I never felt as if I belonged. Can you imagine feeling alone day in and day out in a house or room full of people?

I can. Even at school it seems as if I am the odd one out. In fact this whole town of people freaks me out. Everyone dresses in black and dark morbid colors, hair black or jet black. And dark color eyes. Where I am the opposite to everyone. I am always dressed in bright colors, I have startling eyes, one turquoise blue and one emerald green oval in shape, a cute button nose and the reddest hair you ever saw.

Growing up it seemed strange that my parents always bought me bright beautiful colored clothes. My mother would always kiss my red rosy chubby dimpled cheeks every time she passed by whispering "I wish I could eat you, I wish I could eat you." I always wondered if she just said that as a mother will say to her child or if she meant it literally.

My twin Osmond was a bit like the others except he never spoke one word since he was born, but I was born a chatterbox and could talk your head off if you were not careful. There was always talk and whispers about, but whenever I approached everyone stopped what they were saying or doing, while standing rock still, watching me without blinking an eye; it was an unsettling feeling even at ten years old.

I asked my mother why I was different from everyone else, to which she always replied, while patting my cheeks with those ice-cold hand of hers saying, "You are special Esmerelda and soon you will see how special. Never let anyone intimidate you or make you feel different than who you are. You are my daughter, a part of me. You are who you are and we are who we are," and with a breeze of a kiss on my cheek instead of walking she floated up the stairs never once looking back.

# *Strangers*

I first met Dean not long after my wife Sandra and I split up; it seems like just yesterday. How is it you can be married to someone who you thought was your everything, your better half, your world, and then it's over? It was love at first sight, or back then so I thought. During those years, it seems like we had more down than up times, and more bad days than good ones. Thank God, we had no children. I tried my best, yes, I really did, but I guess sometimes your best is not good enough. And I would not have liked to bring children into this loveless sham of a marriage.

Sandra got me hook, line and sinker as they say. I, being a softie, kind and a fool for love fell right into her trap. Then I learnt what a cold, calculated, heartless bitch she was. I was not about to go another hour or day being around her or in that museum of a house, in which no one can sit here or there, or touch this or that, and plastic had to be on the chairs since they cost about $30,000 a piece.

Oh, didn't I tell you that I was stinking rich? Boy, Sandra sure did her homework on me before she "accidentally" bumped into me on that fateful day.

It was nearing dusk on a sultry, summer night when I moved into my three-and-a-half bathroom condo, on the top floor, with a magnificent view of The Harbor where all the yachts docked. I decided to take a stroll to the local pub called Moonshine, where all the locals hung out or so it seemed. It was a bit downscale, but the food was delicious and the drinks not watered down. Everyone was friendly, very talkative. I was introduced as the new guy in town. I sat on a red bar stool and before I could order a cold Irish draft Guinness, in front of me was the most gorgeous creature I had ever seen in my life. I had to shake my head twice, to make sure this was not a mirage or a figment of my imagination.

I had never been with someone outside of my race, but looking at that chocolate, black haired beauty with the electrifying set of steel grey eyes, I had my stomach in knots and my heart palpitating and I was at a loss for words. Then she said, "I am Dandra, but everyone calls me Dean and I just came over here to tell you we are soul mates and will be married before the month is up. We will have three gorgeous children. And you, my future husband, you will be loved, cherished, not taken for granted. Come on lover boy, it's time for you to buy me a drink." Well, my friends, that was three years ago. We are expecting twins, a boy and a girl. We are so very much in love and family is everything.

# The Drought

Seems like it has not rained in months, which in all actuality it had not: the earth was dry, hard and very coarse. And here were all my pride and joy suffering and hungry. There was a drought, water was scarce and everyone in the neighborhood had to be very careful about their usage of it, but my heart was hurting as my hibiscus, orchids, roses, and other plants and flowers were suffering, and I could not have that. The police had said if they caught anyone using their garden hose that there will be hell to play, plus a $250 fine.

Oh hell no! No one, not even the police told Miss Mabel how and when to run her garden hose, not even the po-po. To hell with those bastards; they better worry about me. Now this here heifer across the street, Mattie, who is as white as they could come, and is as thin as they make them, had the nerve one day to tell me about my excess use of water. Who did this white milk, blonde hair, cake eating all day, television watching ho, who don't even clean her apartment, think she was talking to?

She thinks I don't see the parade of men she be having come through all hours of the day and night. It's a damn shame, is what that is, if you ask me, but hey, no one asked me, so I will just keep my mouth shut. Mattie better be careful and stop minding my beeswax, and think about all what's going in and out and between those skinny, pale tights of hers.

As I was about to close the tap, I heard a shriek and a loud, resounding sound. I stopped and looked around, heard nothing, then went back about my business. Then I heard thud, thud,

thud with a shrill, ear-piercing scream coming from #287, Mattie's apartment. Although I did not want to get involved, I sprinted over, pushed the door open, and walked into the small, cluttered living room, only to see that mongrel Grayson Grey from #3B with his hands raised about to slap Mattie's already crimson cheeks again.

I said, "Sucker, if you know what's good for you, you will put those filthy hands down, and slowly move away from Mattie and get out and stay out, because if I see you sniffing around here again, there will be hell to pay, and be sure to tell Mrs. Grey I said hello."

And that's how I, Mabel the Hershey Chocolate-covered sister, and Mattie, the milk-chocolate sister, as we like to call ourselves, became the best of friends.

*Hattie Middleton*

♦

# My Experience Working for the Board of Education

I started working as a secretary for the New York City Board of Education in 1984 at the Special Education Field Office, District 12 in I.S. 158 located at 800 Home Street in the Bronx. The field office staff consisted of the district administrator, the secretary, two clerical workers, a speech supervisor and a language coordinator. District 12 was responsible for 22 schools. There were seven field supervisors who visited each of the schools to help the special education teachers.

I had numerous responsibilities. I scheduled the times the supervisors would visit each teacher. I also typed up their observations of the teachers. I arranged meetings each month for the supervisors, which included ordering food for them. I ordered supplies for the schools at which the supervisors worked. I disseminated information to the supervisors about Board of Education regulations, school district directives and miscellaneous memoranda. In addition, I helped in the Superintendent's office when the secretary was absent with typing, memos, letters and calling schools to give information to the principals.

The District Office was closed in 2003 because the Mayor at the time felt it would save money. He wanted to run the schools as a business. I and other staff members had to be trained to do a new job: data entry. CAP data entry is a system used for the Individualized Education Plans (IEPs) of special education students.

IEPs are evaluations of a student's strengths and weaknesses as well as goals for them for the next six months or a year. It was very hard for me to learn a new job. I had never done data entry before. However, once I was trained, I found it very interesting to know about the strengths and weaknesses of each student. I told myself I was going to make the best of everything because at that point I had just two and a half more years before I could retire, and that's what I did. In 2006 I completed 25 years of working for the Board of Education (now the Department of Education). I said, "This is it." I said goodbye to everyone. I miss the special education supervisors, teachers and principals. I was sorry to leave some of the special ed students because they had a special place in my heart.

I have now been retired for over 12 years. I am happy doing whatever I want to do whenever I want to do it. I do miss receiving a paycheck every two weeks. I now receive a check once a month and have to budget from that. I would never return to work because retirement is too sweet.

♦

## *That Hat*

It was never good when "a little talk" with mother started out: "It'll be good for you, dear; help develop manual dexterity ...." I tried to fight the impulse—of my eyes, to roll toward my crew cut—but when she added, "and it'll be good for hand/eye coordination, *and* your fine motor skills," even I realized that this was going to be a major snow job...and it wasn't even Thanksgiving!

It was a foregone conclusion, by then, that anything physical—though admittedly, this *was* pushing it—had to be good for a roundish, bookish, increasingly-introverted ten-year-old. Still, I didn't remember ever hearing that I, or anyone I knew of, for that matter, needed remedial work on dexterity and whatever "fine" motor skills were. They sounded vaguely important, and I'm sure seemed to flow naturally, to an adult, from the eye exercises I'd been assigned by an optometrist. Those, along with a dashing pair of tortoise-shell spectacles, *had* helped me progress, after all, from an assessment of "Possibly Mildly Retarded," at an early-fourth-grade parent-teacher conference, to a recommendation, by the same teacher, at the end of that semester, that I be moved into fifth grade.

An "academic promotion" wasn't quite as unusual, then, as it would be, today—except for the fact that mine happened *during Christmas vacation*. How could that not suck, in a one-class/one-room per grade school? At least it wasn't exactly common knowledge, around home, where all the other kids went to public school, while my siblings and I were bussed off to a Catholic school (with imported Irish nuns), in Salt Lake City. Ultimately, It probably didn't make that much difference—I was the kind of "good student/teacher's pet" geek who didn't have many friends in either class, before…or after. At least, I studied a lot—and ultimately got into good colleges— but, talk about delayed gratification!

The "little talk," then, actually turned out to be unvarnished, old-school, stealth-attack parental manipulation: trying (in the '70s) to convince an almost-'tween boy that it was neither as effeminate, nor as embarrassing, as it seemed, to do needlework stuff, at least if it was "good for him," and also "For a Good Cause." Once it became clear that it was inevitable, it actually turned out to be possible to find/create a bonus or two, in the process—as is surprisingly often true, if you can be open to the possibility. In this case, since the starting point for everything was going to be aluminum cans—cut open and hole-punched, based, no doubt, on a pattern in a church-school-teacher's magazine—as the oldest, of the four, I could pull rank, and get to do what seemed (at first) to be the "fun" part, the one with sharp and even potentially "dangerous" equipment. That, also predictably, got to be boring, and _I'd_ manipulate one of my siblings into being excited about it. In addition, since the project involved crocheting around this bendy, metallic "product placement," through the punched holes, to create granny-square-like pieces that could be assembled into nearly any kind of bizarre, and generally useless, thing, though mostly they just became hats—and since baseball caps were easiest, and required fewest squares, they could make the sweatshop worker in each of us feel at least vaguely "productive."

The aluminum provided both a significant amount of surface area—meaning less to be crocheted—*and* opportunities to entertain ourselves by selecting the combination of beverages that would "appear" on each of our creations. Making anything with all beer can sections was my favorite (satisfyingly un-P.C., though that term didn't exist, yet, either), though even I knew that no one in their right mind would dream of wearing such a thing in public. Beer, combined with Pepsi, labels could make a statement, if someone wanted to advertise their non-Mormonness, which may have been tempting—but still nowhere near enough so, to be caught dead in one of those hats.

All this "stuff" was for our annual Church-School Bazaar, which raised money for...actually, I never knew what such an insignificant amount of money could actually be used for. Even thinking about it now, I can't imagine a way that the entire process could have netted anything, all in. Perhaps it was supposed to be about community-building? What my family knew was that, if we made—and contributed—things like beer-can caps (I think I even got bored enough to make a couple of vests—geez, they must'a been hella uncomfortable, *if* anyone ever actually put one on) we'd be absolved of the obligation to participate in the part of the bazaar that involved spending cash—even after making more than a dozen hats, *and vests*, etc., I had to *beg* for enough change to do one spin-paper painting; forget the, indubitably rigged, bottle ring toss or ping-pong ball in the waterglass "games." If any of my siblings knows, even today, it ain't me, how—thousands of miles from any of their families—our parents managed to put four kids—four and a half years between oldest and youngest—through K-8 years of Catholic school. Wait a sec...*those* were benefits of me skipping a year: the tuition—and better yet: the waiting!

What joy there was, in Mudville, for me, mostly derived from imagining my escape—to a coast, another country, or, best of all, another planet (I knew the SciFi section of the local library like the back of my hand). I could work up enough excitement figuring out a way to make a top hat from beer and Pepsi can squares to stay functional...but, taking a clue from the locals, could roll with the tide. The Mormon Church invested in Coca-Cola Bottling of the Mountain West, and its leader had the requisite Dream Vision, so that—though coffee, tea (except "Mormon tea," made from roasted twigs), liquor (heavens!—and mind that plural, there will be a test), cigarettes, and *Pepsi*-Cola products were still prohibited as "pollutants of the body," Coke products became permissible. Rolling with my own realities, that academic promotion became a life preserver, reducing my wait to escape to college—by a year!

# *Still Life*

Objects. Stillness. Life? When is a person an object? Who decides?

Blocks of color, gradationless. I wait. And wonder. And wait. And wait.

When did my life—did I—become this? All surface and solid blocks, without shading, without softening, even at the edges.

Standing. Still. How long? A minute? A generation? The concept of time now seems alien, so personal, with grays and indistinctness and undefined parts that don't fit into a seamless block-solid whole.

This is the fatal incongruity. The mismatch—the cognitive dissonance. Somewhere, I don't know how I could have: I *lost* it? I? Something I did, not something that happened to me? I *became* these blocks of solid colors. I *must* have fought it, at least at first. But was I simply not strong enough ...? Lacking in will ...? Just lazy? Did I care?

People. Strangers. Each one, stranger. Even the once familiar. The family I had no say over. The families I chose. All the strangers—some who even know, or knew, it, but none who ever escaped.

I *am*. I am and my life is still...a still life. Imbued with the details of my observers. I try not to disabuse them. It's just easier, since...why? I can stand still. My still life. And then... No more.

# *Steel*

Steel. Sounds strong. Admirable, even, in a leader—but there's steel and there's *steel*. I have the latter: five to seven pounds of it, on, around and through my spine. There must be a primal reason that so many science fiction aliens—themselves, as parasites, or the hardware they use, to enslave—bond to, and physically integrate with, human spines. It surprised me that the surgeon had to stop what he was doing, and talk himself through rough math, from scratch, when I asked "How much?" He said that no one had ever asked. Really? I wanted to know whether I'd notice anything, getting onto a scale, or into a swimming pool…really! Wouldn't anyone?

It was never *not* going to be a *big deal*, but it didn't really feel like a Big Deal, to a post-grad biochemical engineer, who'd consulted to the medical and pharmaceutical industries. The prospect of attaching erector sets to five cervical (neck) vertebra, and then a dozen more, thoracolumbar (mid-to-lower back), with screws and clamps and 18" steel rods, was clearly something orthopedic surgeons had been doing, for decades—longer, at very least, than the amount of time I'd spent avoiding it, since an "Accountant's Stoop" arthritis diagnosis, in my teens—which didn't, for the record, stop summer vacation construction work, and may have even encouraged my study of ballet, and then music, musical theater and opera.

It's mostly steel, *my* hardware, but includes plastic and titanium parts—all non-magnetic, so I can still get MRIs—and it's all no end of fun at airport security checkpoints these days. The initial surgeries included some cool, hi-tech-sounding stuff, like *Smith-Petersen osteotomies* and *bone-morphogenic protein* (BMP). They also made it seem well-understood; likely to be routine…unremarkable. That's what I wanted. Pre-procedure, I imagined my spine ending up somewhere on a continuum between a "chopped and channeled" tailfin-era Chevy, and a Transformer. That, though, was about as long as the fun would last.

The fusion segments: one from numbers three through seven, cervical—counting down from the top—and the other, from the middle of my chest to the second-lowest (originally) unattached vertebra, just above my hips, meant that there'd be at least two surgeries. Ultimately, I'd have 14—between 2008 and 2016. Each of the "original two" had significant "complications," though nothing of a kind you could sue any-one over (of course, I checked!).

The problems, of course, like in any disaster movie, were foreshadowed. In today's obligatory pre-surgery recita-tions, where you generally ignore the lower-probability "negative outcomes"—I mean, they always include just making the original problem worse—and death. I do remember, though, that all this metal, and its "interfaces" with my bones, "could" provide ideal incubation and hiding spots for bacte-ria—kinda like the back seats of those tailfin Chevys. And, of course, that's exactly what they did for me—but not just *any* bacteria: No, it was—and, yes, I still *live with*—inside-the-bone (courtesy of the BMP) "Methicillin-resistant Staphylococcus Aureus" (MRSA, the "SuperBug").

As you might imagine, my memory of a respectable

chunk of a couple of those years is somewhat fuzzy, but in case I ever forget, pretty much everything significant is still in there. The hardware (V3—even the 18-inch rods; honestly, they'd've done better to install a zipper down the middle of my back, for at least the six-surgery run, from December '08 through November '10); the MRSA; the pain (not insignificantly, the reason I finally agreed to surgery at all) was to prevent/stop/reverse the need for *major* pain meds that my gradual spinal disintegration had finally reached. Lately, I fancy myself a little like Tony Stark, though not exactly as Ironman, but kept alive, on a day to day basis, by the...miracle of modern medical technology? Hardly. Antibiotics and pain meds are actually 19th and 20th Century medicine. Go figure!

And now? *Vessel.* Public monumental sculpture, in the largest land development project in New York City. Arguably "Accessible." The commissioner, and the artist, specified "Disability Accessible"—but not everyone agrees on the result; a "Separate but Equal" elevator is not enough, for some, who envy, I suppose, the people climbing up, down, around and through the whole thing. I don't know who's right. With time, stairs are less and less my friends. On a grander scale, though, the whole thing seems to just be me, inside out: Steel superstructure over around and through which humans walk, ant-like, *and climb stairs*, or ride elevators; and all of it: Done, and too late to really make sense to change now.

# Food Fight

They can be tough—especially in a "no such thing as spoiled food, just spoiled children" kind of home. Part of it is that they can just be difficult for some people to throw out. Even at their very blackest, they can still (arguably) be "for banana bread." And, sometimes, they can be scary. The only time I remember my parents arguing, out loud, in front of us—the four kids—it actually involved a banana, and mother, running out of the house, up the street and out of sight.

For the record, I'm the oldest—and, at the time, I must've been 8 or 9…maybe 10? The youngest is four and a half years younger than me; seems there wasn't much else to do, back when, particularly without money, in the wilds of Utah, so making babies (and caring and paying for them…the irony is rich) was a fairly common recreational activity. Four barely registered as normal, let alone remarkable, or even especially "Catholic," as it would've, most anywhere else, because the Mormons could be such crazy overachievers in that department. It was barely newsworthy for a family to reach a dozen— though it *would* usually make the paper, when a mother and daughter were in a hospital, together, each having a baby. Rah! Probably the most significant "only spoiled children" feature was the fridge. It was, after all, a regular source of friction— between father, and…pretty much anyone. With mother, it was "Why don't you clean this thing out?" With others, more like "what do you *mean* you can't find X?" (usually some kind of chili pepper/hot sauce—he seemed to lose a lot of his sense of taste, along with reason, during his 15ish-year Mid-Life Crisis.)

The door of the fridge, when open, blocked the only passageway between the kitchen and the dining table, and for a (relatively brief) time, father took to sitting on the floor, during a meal, looking for what he wanted. One night, after yelling at each of my brothers in turn, he just sat on the floor, and started scooping armloads of *stuff*—an amazing array of colors, textures, eventually odors—onto the floor. We could hear him, and see a few things, under the door, but he wasn't able to see (or hear) mother get up—we'd been in the middle of dinner—grab the water pitcher, and quietly walk over and empty it onto his head. He didn't react, immediately, but, a few beats later, stood up and winged a totally prize-worthy specimen of blackened banana at mother. It hit the light fixture, and mostly missed her, but she got up, ran for her purse and the door, wasn't fast enough to make both, and ended up walking briskly up the street, after losing a tug-of-war over her purse, with the car keys in it, and just away. We had no clue, where, or for how long.

Father returned, stared at the four of us, and simply said "*finish* your dinners." We had no idea what might happen next: our mother had just "run away," and we all had pretty vivid imaginations. Worse—at least it nearly seemed that way—we were nearly dragged even further into it, ourselves, trying to keep straight faces. As he glared, imperiously, and began to sit down, it was hard to miss the interruption of his movement, as he encountered (and took a moment to identify what we all knew was) the half banana that had landed on his chair.

*Miriam Wexler*

♦

## *What to Think of*

Think of a dream by Henri Rousseau:
A naked woman is reclined on a velvet sofa
which is magically transported to the jungle
on a Persian carpet.

She has fallen asleep and hears the sound of a flute
played by a phantom charmer. The moon shines down.

Painstakingly depicted greens in a colorful palette of oil paint.
In solitude, the princess without a partner and her kiss is to the
    air.
The lions and tigers watch on this island of enchantment.

Think of the lungs of your heart pumping.
Think of the upside down bats coming from a cave at
    nocturne.

Think of a flock of birds flying in a circular motion.
They are naked, too. I greet them almost at sunrise.

Think of fish in a frying pan covered with confetti of many
    shapes and colors.
Think of a circle. Think of heavenly bodies. Think of Rumi.

# Indian Summer

The colors of the day aglow
THE HARVEST, THE HARVEST, THE HARVEST
   THE HARVEST, THE HARVEST
Sparkle purple moon midway in the sky
green, amber, orange, red, mauve, flesh tones of bodies, purple
   and blue
The colors of my life unfold
jubilation
The shamans dance and sing
to heal to meditate to bless to gyrate to circle
MYSTICAL VISION
The purple moon aglow
Remembrancer
Paumanok{Indian name for Long Island}
The sea, the waves with the white caps splashing down and
   kissing the shore.

# A Leprechaun Had a Magical Hat

A leprechaun had a magical hat.
It was not a bat or a cat but a hat.
It was green with flowers on the rim, with trim.

The country folks put their hands into the mystical hat.
There were jewels in the hat.
In truth it was a pot of gold.

The purple moon shone from above
and glimmers of bright light emanated from the sky
so high, so high, so high.

Meanwhile, on the pavement in Chelsea
the folks wished that they were
back in Dublin, in their heart of hearts.

## *Starry Night*

The sky is ablaze, vibrant, luminous.

Look at the amber moon dancing across the summer sky
Peeking its glow behind blue-purple clouds.
Look at dripping beeswax drizzled over heavenly clouds.

Like this
The rapture of the universe unfolds swirling above.

Like this
Vincent Van Gogh's Starry Night is magically present.

If only I could touch you, my friend.

Like this
The stars unraveling mystical, majestic and luminous.
The engulfing snake-like cypress is a door to your world
    beyond.

The stars come spinning. The moon overlooking
The peaceful French-Dutch village below.

## *Silence*

The moment is all there is.
Life is finite.
The full amber moon with its shadows—
I can almost touch it.
Is it truth or fantasy?

.
.
.
.

I am happy in spite of overwhelming
Obstacles for me and my loves
In this incredible universe.

We are here.

.
.
.
.

Emmanuel, the morning star.

Be.

## *Thunderbird Lake Where*
## *Everything is Possible*

I dreamed I was afloat
on Thunderbird Lake.
Alone, alone on a little boat
on Thunderbird Lake
where everything is possible.

Waves crashing.

I dreamed he was alone, afloat
on a raft on Thunderbird Lake
where everything is possible.

Today we are alone, afloat
on a little boat on Thunderbird Lake
where the impossible is possible.

# *Early Memories of My Childhood at Coney Island*

Asleep
Walking down the boardwalk
into water
foam below
the heavens
with sunburst
above orange sun

Reminiscence
a splinter in my right thumb
pain unspoken pain
the nurse stepped on my foot
so my splintered thumb
would not hurt as much
she gave me a lollipop
what I wanted was
cotton candy
stuff your feelings
where your dreams are hidden

# SONGS

I.

There are places in my home full of old photographs, I almost
    never want to see them again.
Remembrance of my past brings unbearable pain.
Like dead hyacinths on fire.
I turn the photos around so I do not see their faces.

Then their souls reach out to me.
Female, hexed at birth with a neurological impairment.
Why was this always a secret, always a secret?

Today, time is draining from the hourglass.
There is much, so much I missed out on.
My mom and dad and that space in time
Made things much worse.

II.

Mom and Daddy appeared to the world as good parents
 and I appeared as a monster.
 In truth, I was dying on the inside, like bleeding hearts afire.
 Daddy was macho, unable to be a father to a daughter who was
    blemished.

But the dark green and deep brown, square house on the dead-
    end street

where I spend my adolescence and a part of my adulthood
were dead space, like decapitated daisies
from Prospect Park.
Another day, ennui, ennui.

III.
*To the souls of my parents*

I thank you for not giving me a lobotomy, like our neighbor
    Charlie or ECT.

Today, I have grown strong because of twenty-two plus years
    of therapy and hard work with my therapist.

WOULD YOU DO THINGS IN THE SAME WAY AGAIN?
THE ANSWER IS LOST IN TRANSLATION

NEVERTHELESS, I FORGIVE BOTH OF YOU
The past is the past, tomorrow is now and I choose to strive
    forward and dance.

IV.
From this day forward I am wedded to the sky
                    *for Faye*

Twins merged with the sky, between heaven and earth.
Here, beyond Michelangelo and the Sistine Chapel,
Images of G-D touching the hand of man—
the psyche and the soul.

Birds fly above the earth toward G-D and eternity.
They fly high, high, high above the clouds.
Birds fly in a circular motion.
They pass the seagulls
Beyond the nimbus clouds above the rainbow.

Here beyond what is visible and what is invisible.
Faye is a Gemini


V.
*for my father*

Passionately he doffs the farm team hat
and runs around the bases: he is a baseball hitter.
A home run happens; like Icarus, it flies near the sun.
The crowd is wild with madness and frenzy…
a total chaos and pandemonium.
Daddy-O

# Acknowledgements

We share our belief that the world is a better place when everyone's voice is listened to and respected.

Many thanks go to our foundation, government, and corporate supporters, without whom this writing community and publication would not exist: Amazon Literary Partnership, Cowan Slavin Foundation, Emmanuel Baptist Church Benevolence Fund, Meringoff Family Foundation, The National Endowment for the Arts, The New York City Department of Cultural Affairs, and the Two West Foundation. NYWC programming is also made possible by the New York State Council on the Arts with the support of Governor Andrew Cuomo and the New York State Legislature.

We rely heavily on the support of individual NYWC members and attendees of our annual Write-A-Thon and Red & Black Fundraiser. In addition, the members of our Board of Directors have kept this vital, rewarding work going year after year: Louise Crawford, Atiba Edwards, Marian Fontana, Kaitlyn Greenidge, Susan Karwoska, Brooke McCaffrey, Sophie McManus, Alexis Nixon, and NYWC Founder and Executive Director Aaron Zimmerman. We would also like to thank the staff at CIDNY.

To find out more how you can sponsor a NYWC publication or program, please contact info@nywriterscoalition.org or (718) 398-2883.

NY Writers Coalition

NY Writers Coalition Inc. (NYWC) is a 501(c)(3) non-profit
organization that creates opportunities for formerly voiceless
members of society to be heard through the art of writing.

One of the largest community-based writing organizations in
the country, NYWC provides free, unique, and powerful
creative writing workshops throughout New York City for
people from groups that have been historically deprived of
voice in our society, including at-risk and disconnected
youth, homeless and formerly homeless persons, individuals
who are or have been incarcerated, veterans of war, those
living with disabilities, cancer, and other major illnesses,
immigrants, seniors, and many others.

For more information about NYWC programs
and NY Writers Coalition Press publications visit
www.nywriterscoalition.org

Made in the USA
Middletown, DE
10 March 2019